This
Treasure Cove Story
belongs to

_____

EYE OF THE DRAGON

A CENTUM BOOK 978-1-911460-73-2
Published in Great Britain by Centum Books Ltd.
This edition published 2019.

1 3 5 7 9 10 8 6 4 2

© 2019 MARVEL. All Rights Reserved.

Centum Books Ltd, 20 Devon Square, Newton Abbot,
Devon, TQ12 2HR, UK.

www.centumbooksltd.co.uk | books@centumbooksltd.co.uk
CENTUM BOOKS Limited Reg. No. 07641486.

A CIP catalogue record for this book is available
from the British Library.

Printed in China.

centum

A Treasure Cove Story

MARVEL
THE INVINCIBLE
IRON MAN

EYE OF THE DRAGON

Based on the stories by Marvel Comics
By Billy Wrecks
Illustrated by Patrick Spaziante

World-famous inventor Tony Stark is the guest of honour at a festival in New York City's Chinatown. Tony cuts a ribbon and starts the parade. Fireworks pop, dancers twirl and acrobats leap.

A parade float pulled by Chinese dragons rolls down the street. The dancers underneath the colourful, sparkling dragon costumes make them twist and curl like giant snakes.

The float carries a priceless gem called the Eye of the Dragon. The gem will go on display in a museum when the parade is over. Tony and the crowd cheer as it passes by.

Suddenly, the villain known as the Mandarin appears! He is armed with ten powerful energy rings.

'The Eye of the Dragon will be mine!' the Mandarin exclaims as he uses his Ice Blast ring to freeze the parade float in its tracks.

Tony Stark runs to an alley. Hidden in his briefcase is
powerful high-tech armour that he puts on to become...

THE INVINCIBLE IRON MAN!

Armoured up, Iron Man flies into action!

'Stop right there!' Iron Man commands.
The sinister Mandarin looks up to see
who would dare challenge him.

'Iron Man!' the Mandarin growls as he grabs the gem. He fires a beam of energy at the hero, but Iron Man's armour deflects the blast.

'Your armour cannot withstand the might of my rings for long,' the Mandarin boasts. 'Each one is more than a match for you!'

The Mandarin uses his Vortex ring
to create a twisting tornado. It sends
Iron Man spinning around and around.

WHOOOOSH!

'Is that all you've got?' Iron Man says.

The Mandarin laughs triumphantly. Electricity crackles from his Electro-Blast ring.

ZZZZZAP!

Iron Man scoops up a handful of fireworks and tosses them into the air. The Mandarin's electricity ignites the fireworks.

'Arrrghh!' the Mandarin cries out as the fireworks go off and light up the sky.

POP!

POP!

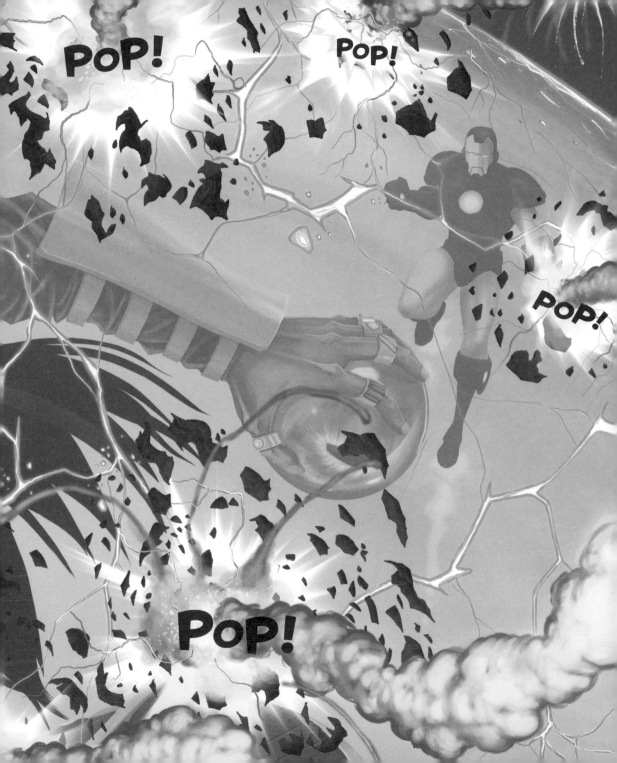

'Now it's time to wrap things up,' Iron Man says, grabbing one of the long parade dragons.

Iron Man ties the Mandarin up tight.
The villain can't use his rings.

'The Eye of the Dragon is for everyone to enjoy,' Iron Man tells the Mandarin. 'It's not just for you.'

Iron Man fires his repulsor beams into the air,
and they explode like fireworks. Everyone cheers.

GO, IRON MAN!

Treasure Cove Stories

Book list may be subject to change.